W9-CNI-029

This book belongs to:

....

....

Editor: Lucy Cuthew
Designer: Hannah Mason
Series Editor: Ruth Symons
Editorial Director: Victoria Garrard
Art Director: Laura Roberts-Jensen

First published in the United States by QEB Publishing, Inc.
3 Wrigley, Suite A, Irvine, CA 92618

www.qed-publishing.co.uk

A CIP record for this book is available from the Library of Congress.

ISBN 978 1 60992 708 0

Printed in China

Blow Your Nose, BIG BAD WOLF

Written by Steve Smallman
Illustrated by Bruno Merz

QEB Publishing

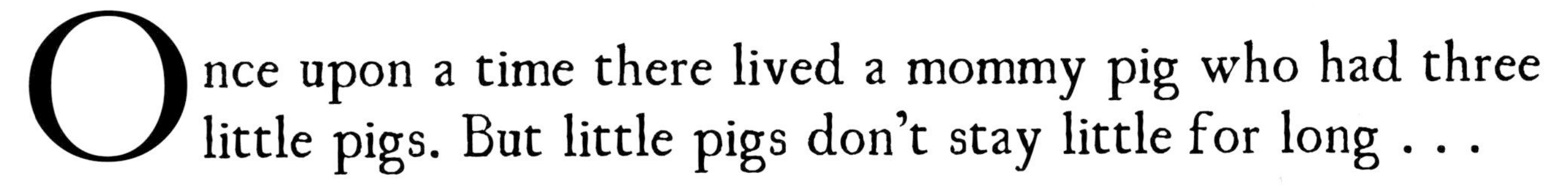

Once upon a time there lived a mommy pig who had three little pigs. But little pigs don't stay little for long . . .

Mommy Pig gave the pigs
some money and a box
of tissues each, and sent
them on their way.

The first little pig met a girl
with a wagon full of straw.

So he bought the straw,

The second little pig met a man
with a wagon full of sticks.

So she bought the sticks,

The third little pig met a family
with a wagon full of bricks.

So he bought the bricks,

built himself a house,

and went inside for a nice nap.

built herself a house,

and went inside to watch TV.

built himself a house,

and went inside for a snack.

There was a wolf who lived nearby. His name was Big Bad, but he was really nice!

Big Bad had a nasty cold with a horrible runny nose. What he needed was a tissue to blow his nose with.

He was on his way to buy some, when he saw a new straw house.

He peeped through the window and saw a little pig with a **big box of tissues!**

Big Bad knocked politely
on the door and said,

"Little pig, little pig,
let me come in."

"Not by the hair on my chinny-chin-chin!"
squealed the little pig.

"Oh, please!" sniffled Big Bad, "all I want is . . .

A-A-A-A-TISSUE!"

Big Bad sneezed a sneeze so big that it blew down the house of straw!

"Eeek!" squealed the little pig, and he ran next door.

Big Bad followed him to the house of sticks.
He knocked politely on the door and said,

"Little pigs, little pigs,
let me come in."

"Not by the hair on our chinny-chin-chins!"
squealed the two little pigs.

"Oh, please," sniffled Big Bad,
"all I want is . . .

A-A-A-A-TISSUE!"

And he sneezed a gigantic, snotty sneeze. It was so gigantic that it blew down the house of sticks!

"Yuck!" squealed the little pigs, and they ran next door.

Big Bad followed them to the house of bricks.
He knocked politely on the door and said,

"Little pigs, little pigs,
let me come in."

"Not by the hair on our chinny-chin-chins!"
squealed the three little pigs.

"Oh, don't be mean,"
sniffled Big Bad,
"all I want is . . .
A-A-A-A-TISSUE!"

And he sneezed the biggest, snottiest, slimiest sneeze he had ever sneezed. But the house of bricks did not blow down!

The three little pigs were delighted!
They danced around singing:

"We've got tissues, you've got none.
You're the sneezy, snotty one!"

And that's when Big Bad got really mad!

"Then I'll come down the chimney and get a tissue myself!" he roared.

But as he started climbing up the drainpipe . . .

. . . the three little pigs put a cauldron of water on the fire!

"If Big Bad Snot-Face Wolf comes down here," they chuckled,

"we'll **boil** his bottom!"

But Big Bad was so quick that when he came tumbling down the chimney, he landed in a cauldron of nice, warm water.

With a **big splash**, the fire went out.

"Please don't gobble us up!" squealed the three little pigs.

"I don't want to eat you," sniffled Big Bad.

"I just needed . . .

A-TISSUE!"

And before he could
cover his mouth,
he sneezed a big wet
sneeze all over the
three little pigs.

"Gross!"
they all cried.

If only they had given Big Bad a tissue,
they wouldn't have caught his cold!

The pigs passed around the tissues and
made sure they passed some to the wolf.

Big Bad settled down in his nice warm bath,
blew his nose and started to feel much better.

Next steps

Show the children the cover again. When they first saw it did they think that they already knew this story? How is this story different from the other story? Which parts are the same?

At the beginning of the story one of the little pigs sneezes everywhere and his mommy tells him off. Everyone sneezes, so what has the pig done wrong?

Ask the children if they have ever had a cold. Do they use a tissue when they sneeze? Why is it important?

The wolf is usually a baddie in the traditional story. Ask the children what they think of Big Bad. Do they think he is nasty or nice? Does Big Bad blow down the houses on purpose?

Ask the children what they think of the three little pigs. What do the children think would have happened if the first little pig had given Big Bad a tissue?

Ask the children to draw a picture from the story. Which picture have they chosen? What is happening in the picture?